Rainforests

Michelle Vasiliu

NELSON
A Cengage Company

Australia • Brazil • Japan • Korea • Mexico • Singapore • Spain • United Kingdom • United States

Rainforests

Text: Michelle Vasiliu
Editor: Vanessa Pellatt
Design: Karen Mayo
Series design: James Lowe
Photo researcher: Libby Henry
Production controller: Adam Bextream
Reprint: Jennifer Foo

Acknowledgements
The author and publisher would like to acknowledge permission to reproduce material from the following sources:
Auscape/Biosphoto/Cyril Ruoso: p. 8 (bottom); Auscape/Steven David Miller: p. 7 (inset); Corbis Australia: pp. 1, 9 (top), 10 (inset), 18, cover; Fairfax Photos/Rick Stevens: p. 15; Getty Images: pp. 7 (main), 16 (fruit), 17, 19; iStockphoto/Morley Read: pp. 6 (main), back cover; Kylie Nicholls © Cengage Learning Australia: pp. 4–5; Lonely Planet Images/Richard I'Anson: p. 14; Photolibrary: pp. 3, 6 (cassowary), 6 (orchid), 8 (top), 9 (bottom), 10 (main), 11 (inset), 11 (main), 12, 13, 20, 21, 22, 23; Shutterstock/Benis Arapovic: p.16 (sugar); Shutterstock/Elena Elisseeva: p. 16 (corn); Shutterstock/Paul Paladin: p. 16 (chocolate).

Every effort has been made to trace and acknowledge copyright. However, if any infringement has occurred, the publishers tender their apologies and invite the copyright holders to contact them.

Fast Forward Independent Texts
Level 21

For product information and technology assistance,
in Australia call 1300 790 853;
in New Zealand call 0508 635 766

For permission to use material from this text or product,
please email **aust.permissions@cengage.com**

ISBN 978 0 17 017937 9
ISBN 978 0 17 017899 0 (set)

Cengage Learning Australia
Level 7, 80 Dorcas Street
South Melbourne, Victoria Australia 3205

Cengage Learning New Zealand
Unit 4B Rosedale Office Park
331 Rosedale Road, Albany, North Shore NZ 0632

For learning solutions, visit **cengage.com.au**

Printed in Australia by Ligare Pty Ltd
3 4 5 6 7 8 9 22 21 20 19 18

Rainforests

Michelle Vasiliu

Contents

CHAPTER 1

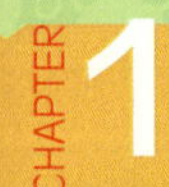

Types of Rainforests

Rainforests get over 1300 millimetres of rain a year.

When people think of rainforests, they might imagine them to be very hot and humid. These are tropical rainforests and they can be found near the equator.

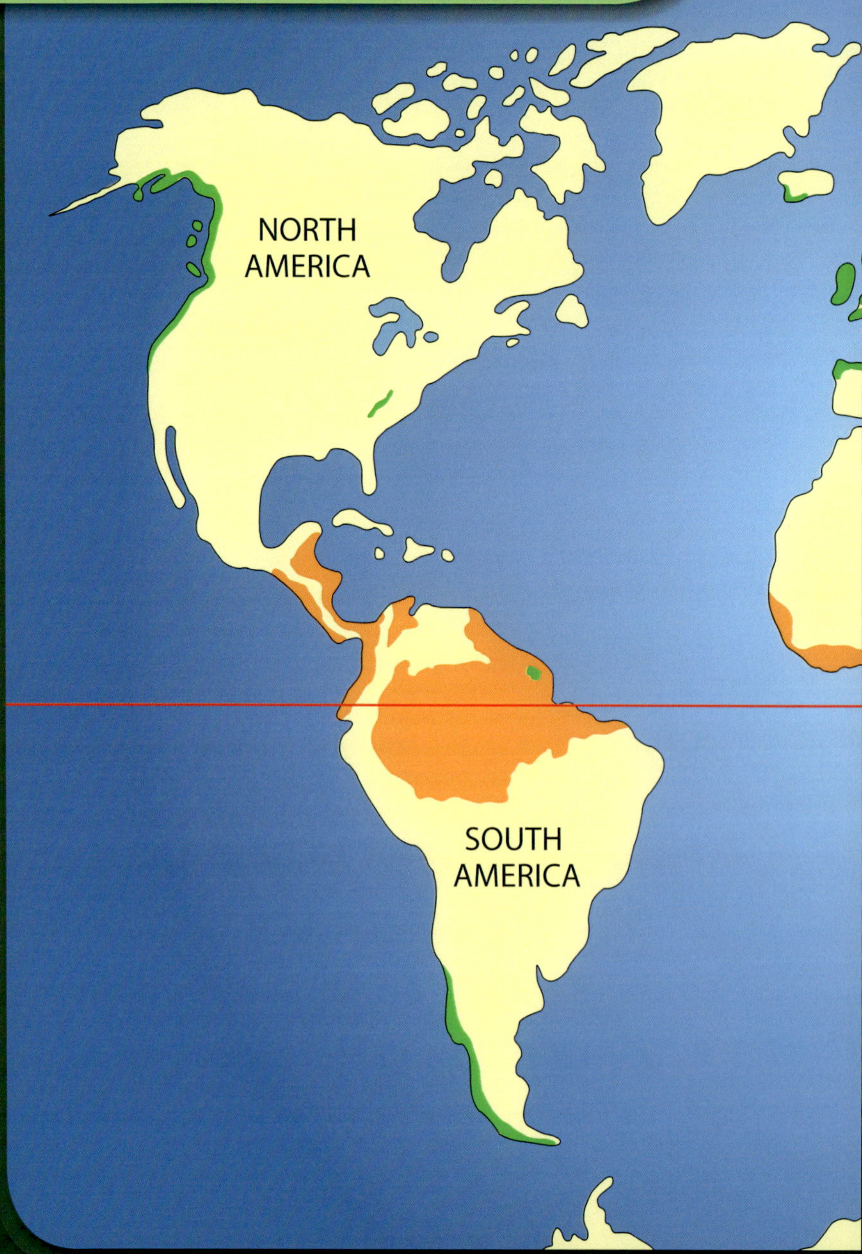

NORTH AMERICA
SOUTH AMERICA

But there is another kind of rainforest, called a temperate rainforest. Temperate rainforests are found further away from the equator.

It rains almost every day in both tropical and temperate rainforests.

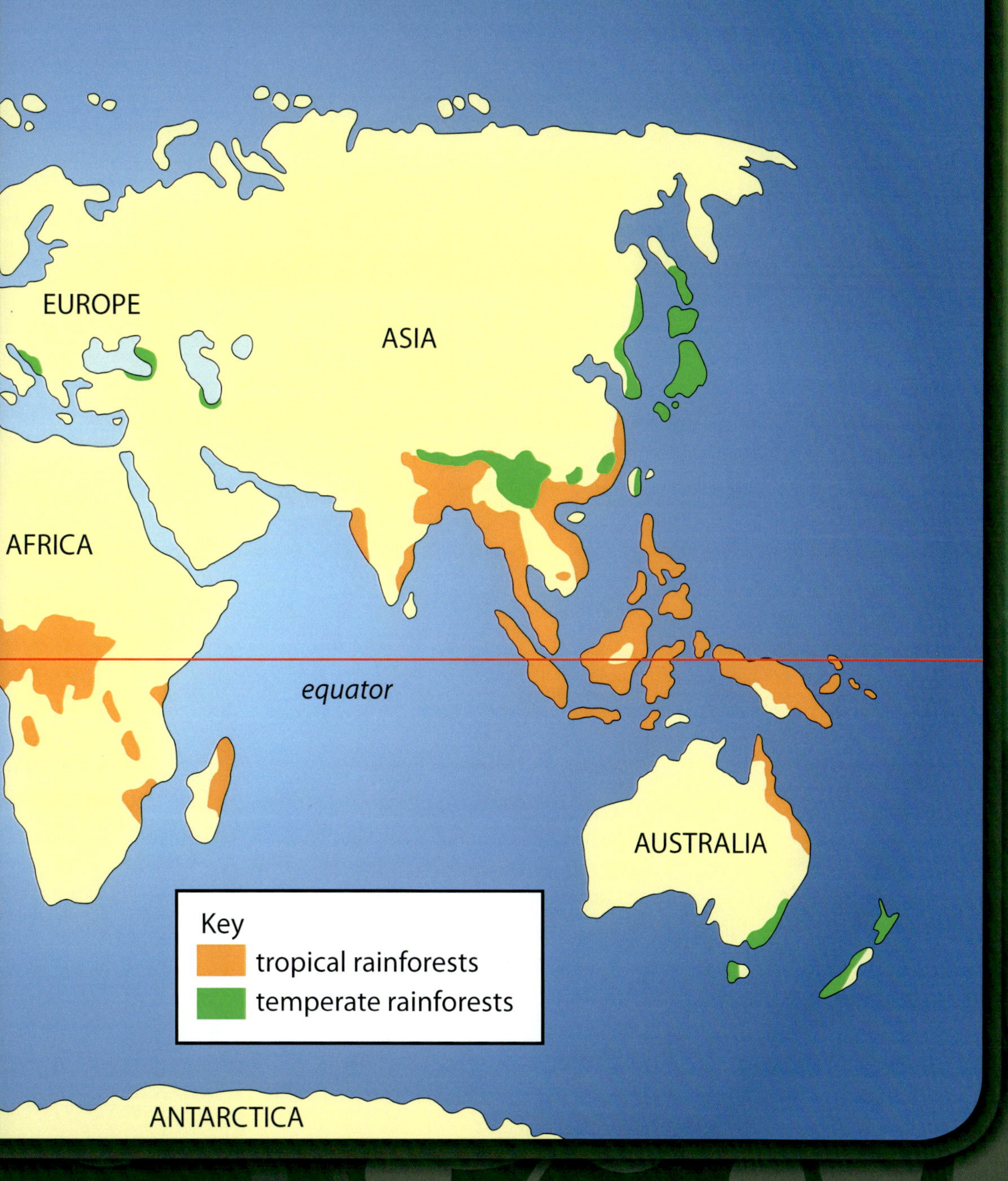

Tropical Rainforests

Tropical rainforests grow in areas where it is warm all year round.

These types of rainforests have very rich **ecosystems**, with many kinds of plants and animals living together.

The cassowary can be found in the rainforests of New Guinea and north-eastern Australia.

This orchid grows in the rainforests of South America.

Tropical rainforests are home to more than half of the animal and plant **species** in the world.

strangler fig vine, Indonesia

The Ulysses butterfly is most commonly found in the tropical rainforests of Australia.

Tropical rainforests have four main layers.
The upper canopy is at the top.

The next layer is called the canopy.
There is plenty of food in this layer
so this is where most of the animals live.

*flying foxes,
upper canopy, Australia*

*northern woolly spider monkey,
canopy, Brazil*

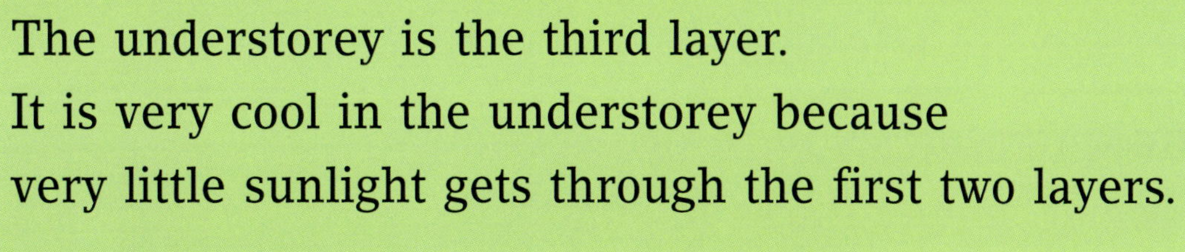

The understorey is the third layer.
It is very cool in the understorey because very little sunlight gets through the first two layers.

The rainforest floor is at ground level.
Almost no sunlight reaches the rainforest floor so only a few plants grow in this area.

golden eyelash viper, understorey, Central and South America

The world's largest flower, the *Rafflesia arnoldii*, can be found on the forest floor in the rainforests of Indonesia.

Temperate Rainforests

Temperate rainforests have two seasons, with warmer temperatures in summer and cooler temperatures in winter.

elk, North America

The cool winter temperatures limit the number of species that can live in a temperate rainforest.

black currawong, Tasmania, Australia

Temperate rainforests have three main layers.
The canopy is at the top,
the understorey is in the middle,
and a layer of plants grows on the forest floor.

Most of the animals in a temperate rainforest live on or near the ground, where there is lots of food.

Here, the trees shelter the animals from the Sun, wind and rain.

black bear, North America

CHAPTER 2

Rainforests and the Atmosphere

All rainforests are important to life on Earth because they affect the **atmosphere**.

As trees grow,
they take in carbon dioxide
and release oxygen back into the air.
People and animals then breathe in the oxygen.
It is believed that 40 per cent of the world's oxygen comes from rainforests.

Changes to the rainforests can also change weather patterns. Rainforests are often cleared by burning down the trees. Carbon dioxide and other gases are then released into the atmosphere where they trap warm air. Scientists believe that this is making the world warmer and could be causing more storms, floods and tornadoes.

flooding in Narrabri, Australia, 1998

CHAPTER 3

Rainforests and People

Many of the things that people eat or use come from tropical rainforests.

At least 80 per cent of the **developed** world's food comes from plants that are native to tropical rainforests. Now these plants are grown in places all over the world.

These foods come from plants originally found in rainforests.

Many different medicines are also made from rainforest plants. Yet less than one per cent of rainforest plants have been tested to see if they could work as medicines. There could be many more rainforest plants with healing properties.

Rainforest **timber** is used for fuel and to make houses, furniture, clothes and paper.
People also mine for oil and metals under the rainforests.

These logs have come from rainforest trees.

CHAPTER 4

Threats to Rainforests

The greatest threat to rainforests is from people.

Trees from rainforests are cut down
and the timber is sold to developed countries.
This is one of the biggest causes of rainforest destruction.

Sometimes, rainforest areas are cleared
to make room for roads, houses and farms.
In Brazil, over a third of the rainforest has been destroyed
to make way for crops and cattle farms.

Trees that are hundreds of years old are cut down for their wood or to make way for farms.

Animals that live in rainforests are also under threat. Some animals are hunted even though it is against the law. As the rainforests are destroyed, more animals are losing their homes.

It is estimated that only about 15 000 jaguars remain in the wild because of **deforestation** and illegal hunting.

Orangutans cannot survive if logging continues in Indonesia.

Rainforest plants and animals make up an ecosystem.
When too many animals are killed
or too many trees are cut down,
a part of the rainforest ecosystem is also destroyed.
Already nearly half of the world's rainforests have been lost.
Some scientists think that if people do not start
looking after the rainforests,
there will not be any left in the next 40 years.

5

Rainforests and the Future

Many of the world's rainforests are millions of years old.
Some of the most ancient plants in the world grow in these rainforests.
It is important that they are protected.

Australia, Antarctica, Africa, South America and New Zealand were once joined together as a landmass called Gondwana. Flora from Gondwana can still be found in Tasmania's rainforests.

Developed countries use rainforest timber to make products such as furniture and paper. These trees take hundreds of years to grow and when one tree is cut down, many of the plants around it also die. One way to stop this from happening is to plant special forests to use for timber instead of using the rainforest trees.

A lot of outdoor furniture is made from rainforest timber.

People could also sell **renewable** resources such as plant products, which could then be used to make medicines and food. These products could be grown **sustainably**.

Without the rainforests,
many plants and animals will die.
The environment, atmosphere and weather patterns
will change forever.
To protect the rainforests,
people should stop cutting down trees for timber or farming.

These coffee beans came from plants that are farmed sustainably.

People around the world can help to save the rainforests by

- supporting organisations that work to protect rainforests
- not buying products that are made from rainforest timber
- trying to buy products that are not made by destroying rainforests.

Glossary

atmosphere the gases surrounding Earth

deforestation the removal of trees

developed industrialised or advanced

ecosystems communities of plants and animals

renewable able to be replaced over time

species a group of plants or animals that are the same

sustainably grown in a way that does not damage the natural environment

timber wood

Index